Fair

A Cherrytree Book

Designed and produced by A S Publishing

First published 1996
by Cherrytree Press Ltd
327 High St
Slough
Berkshire SL1 1TX

First published in paperback 2002
Copyright this edition © Evans Brothers Limited 2002

British Library Cataloguing in Publication Data
Amos, Janine
    Fair - (Viewpoints)
    1. Fairness - Juvenile literature 2. Moral development
    Juvenile literature
    I. Title
    155.4'1825

ISBN 1 84234 147 2

Printed in Spain by G. Z. Printek

Fair

Two stories seen from two points of view

by Janine Amos
Illustrated by Gwen Green

CHERRYTREE BOOKS

Laura at the campsite

Laura woke up. The tent was filled up with a dim, yellow light. The other girls were still asleep. Laura could hear them breathing. She felt hot and sticky. Outside, a bird sang on and on.

"It's morning," thought Laura, "and first day of camp!"

Very quietly, she wriggled into her jeans. Then, pulling on a sweatshirt and jacket, she crawled into the open air. The campsite was quiet. Laura was the only one awake.

"Great! A chance to explore all by myself," she thought, and she set off across the field.

In the next field, Laura found a pond. There was a lot of green weed on top, but the water was clear. Laura crouched down and peered at the surface.

The pond was full of life. Water beetles scurried about alongside great clouds of frogspawn. Laura sat for ages watching a dragonfly. At last, her tummy rumbled and she headed back to the tents.

Laura gobbled down her cereal. Mrs Crocker her teacher was telling everyone the plans for the day.

"Washing up… tidying … making sandwiches … pony trekking at eleven o'clock."

Laura wasn't really listening. She was thinking about the pond.

"I'll just have time for another visit if I hurry," she thought. She dropped her dirty bowl on to the pile and slipped away.

Laura enjoyed jogging about the hillside on the pony's back. The spring sunshine felt good on her shoulders. And she could smell the pony's warm, oaty breath.

At lunchtime, they stopped for a rest. Someone had made cheese sandwiches. As Laura bit into hers, she thought again about her secret pond. The second time she went, she had seen a brown furry animal plop into the water.

That evening before supper, Laura took out her notebook. Mrs Crocker had asked the girls to keep a diary.

"I'll call it my Nature Notebook," thought Laura, inking in the title. "I'll start with The Pond."

Outside the tent, someone was calling her name.

"Let them manage without me," muttered Laura. "I'm far too busy."

The next morning, Laura sat watching the pond. Suddenly she saw Sally, Jo and Sophie.

Laura smiled. "Look at the newts and frogspawn!" said Laura.

"We don't care about them!" snapped Sophie. "Go and do some work for a change. We're doing everything. It's not fair!"

Laura felt two red patches burning on her cheeks. She didn't know what to say.

To read Sophie's side of things, turn to page 18.

Tom and the strawberries

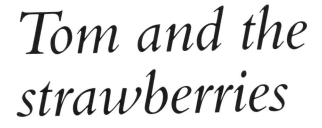

Laura, Tom, Jack and Annie were
all on holiday. They were staying at
Gran and Grandad's in the country.
Every year, Gran planned plenty of
things to do.

"Tomorrow it's strawberry-
picking," she reminded them.

"Yippee!" shouted Tom. He
loved strawberries.

The next morning, straight after breakfast, they set off. Grandad drove slowly along the winding country lanes.

It was stuffy in the car. The sun was streaming in through the windscreen. Tom's T-shirt was sticking to his back.

At last they arrived at the old farm. The children knew the way and raced off to start picking.

"Keep your hats on," warned Gran. "The sun is very strong and it's hot work."

Tom knelt down and lifted the leaves for his first glimpse of strawberries. There were loads of them, bright, juicy red against the green leaves. Delicious!

Tom had the first strawberry halfway to his mouth when Gran appeared.

"Tom!" she boomed. "You know you mustn't eat them until they've been washed!"

Gran was afraid of the chemical sprays. Tom groaned and dropped the strawberry into his container.

It was hard work picking in the hot sun. Tom felt it shining on the back of his neck. But he picked as fast as he could. And soon his container was almost full.

Laura started to grumble. She burned easily, and the strawberry field had no shade.

After a while, Gran called them to stop.

"That's enough!" she declared. "Home now, before we all melt. It's not worth getting sunstroke for strawberries."

Back at the house, Gran tipped all the strawberries into a huge bowl and washed them.

"These will be lovely," she said, carrying them away. "There will be just enough for lunch."

Tom wrinkled up his nose. He wanted to eat them now. Instead he went outside to play with Jack and Annie until lunch. They started a game of rounders, but it was too hot, and they flopped under a tree.

Tom grew tired of the garden and wandered inside. The table was already set for the children's lunch. On the dresser was the bowl of strawberries.

Tom looked around. No one would miss a few! He helped himself to one. It tasted really good. He took some more, and some more, and some more. Before long he felt full.

Tom looked at the bowl in disbelief. There were hardly any strawberries left!

What would the others say? Tom listened to the clock going tock, tock, tock. He watched a bee buzzing against the window. His heart began to hammer. He felt awful.

Then Tom heard voices. Where could he hide? But his cousins were already coming into the room. Guilty, he wiped his sticky mouth with the back of his hand, and waited.

*For the others'
point of view,
go to page 24.*

Sophie at the campsite

Sophie sat up in her sleeping bag and rubbed her eyes. She smiled across to Sally and Jo.

"Where's Laura?" asked Sally. No one knew.

They heard Mrs Crocker their teacher calling. "Time to get up! Breakfast!"

Soon Mrs Crocker was passing round cereal packets and breakfast bowls. Sophie spotted Laura running across the field.

"I'll save some for Laura," said Sophie, reaching for a clean bowl.

After breakfast, Mrs Crocker gave out a list of jobs.

"At camp we all work together," said the teacher. "Two people from a tent wash up, two tidy up, and everyone helps to make sandwiches. Then we can all go pony trekking!"

Sophie thought that sounded fair.

Inside the tent, Sally and Jo were tidying up.

"You and Laura can do the washing up. OK?" said Sally.

"OK," nodded Sophie. But Laura wasn't around. So Sophie did the washing up on her own.

Laura came back just in time for the trekking. Sophie went up to her.

"Where did you go?" asked Sophie. "I've made your sandwiches for lunch, anyway."

Laura just smiled and nodded. Sophie could see she wasn't even listening.

By that evening, after a long pony ride and a long nature walk, the girls were tired. Everyone was hungry. "If you want to eat, pitch in!" laughed Mrs Crocker.

Sally and Jo were sent to fetch water. Sophie and Laura were supposed to make the salad. But Laura had gone again. So Sophie did it on her own. She felt a bit cross.

Laura appeared just as the food was ready. Everyone enjoyed supper, and afterwards Mrs Crocker played her guitar.

At last when the singing was over, it was time to wash up.

"It must be Laura's turn to do that," said Sally. But Laura wasn't there.

The next morning after breakfast, the girls had to make a picnic lunch and tidy the tents. Laura headed off to the pond.

"All this work, that's the worst of camping!" groaned Sally.

"It doesn't really take long, if everyone helps," said Jo, zipping up a sleeping bag.

"But they don't!" Sophie pointed out. "Laura never does her share. Let's make her tidy the tent!"

The three girls set off across the field to find Laura.

"She always goes this way," said Sophie.

As they went, they talked about Laura.

"She hasn't done one thing to help out so far," said Sally.

Sophie nodded. "She only cares about herself," she decided. "She thinks she's above everyone else!"

They found Laura sitting in the grass. She was smiling.

Sophie could feel herself bubbling up inside. She began to shout. "You're lazy and selfish! It's just not fair!"

Laura and the strawberries

Laura pulled her sun hat down over her face. Riding in the back of Grandad's car always made her feel sick. Laura didn't mind picking strawberries but today was really too hot. She knew they were only going because Gran had promised Tom. He was her favourite.

Laura closed her eyes, trying to think of cool things. And the car went on its bumpy way.

At the strawberry fields it was hotter than ever. There were no trees, just rows and rows of strawberry plants.

Laura picked and picked. Her nails and fingers were stained red with juice. Her knees were dusty with brown earth, but her container was full to the very top.

Laura felt the strong sun beating down on her. She felt dizzy and her face burned.

Back in the car, Laura kept very still and quiet. She couldn't wait to lie down in her cool bedroom. Tom and Annie sang "Ten Green Bottles" loudly all the way.

After a rest, Laura felt better. She went into the garden to look for the others. She sat down with Jack and Annie under the trees. The children watched a line of ants scurrying along the path.

"They don't mind the heat!" said Jack.

"They haven't been kneeling down picking strawberries for an hour!" replied Laura, smiling.

The best thing about strawberry picking is eating them afterwards!" said Annie. "I hope we picked enough."

Laura laughed. "It's nearly lunchtime now," she said. "I wonder where Tom is?"

Laura, Jack and Annie went in through the french windows. The smell of strawberries filled the room. Tom stood by the table, looking at his feet.

"You've been eating them!" Laura screamed at her brother.

Jack picked up the bowl.

"What! You've stuffed yourself!" he shouted.

"You pig!" screeched Annie.

Laura couldn't believe it. Nearly a whole bowl of strawberries. How could he? She went hot all over. She felt herself beginning to shake.

"It's just not fair!" she raged. "All that picking! What about us? I hate you!"

Laura was boiling with anger. But the strawberries were gone.

Sophie says

"Laura didn't do her fair share. I suppose she thinks she's too good to do boring jobs. Other people had to work harder because of her. But she doesn't care."

Laura says

"I'm sorry. I was unfair. I was so interested in the secret pond, I forgot to join in the work. But I wasn't trying to be better than anyone else. I just didn't think."

Tom says

"I didn't mean to eat all the strawberries. I was only going to eat my share. Then I got carried away. I'll never do it again. I promise."

Laura says

"It was so unfair of Tom. We all picked the strawberries. And we deserved an equal share. He just sneaked in and helped himself. He's greedy and selfish."

BEING FAIR

Laura forgot to be fair. She was having such a good time, she forgot to think of anyone else.

Tom didn't mean to be selfish, either. It's sometimes easy to get carried away doing just what you like. But that's not fair.

Fairness is about sharing with other people. It might mean sharing things, like food or toys. Or it might mean sharing hard work and boring jobs. Fairness means taking turns.

Fairness is about caring, too. Being fair means caring enough about others to remember how they might be feeling. Has anyone ever been unfair to you? Try to remember how that made you feel. It will help you to be fair in the future. And learning to be fair is an important part of growing up.